THE FINAL REBOUND

(You haven't lived life, until you've appreciated it)

DeVon D. Cooper Sr.

PublishAmerica
Baltimore

First printing

All characters in this book are fictitious, and any resemblance to real persons, living or dead, is coincidental.

PublishAmerica has allowed this work to remain exactly as the author intended, verbatim, without editorial input.

Softcover 9781630000776
PUBLISHED BY PUBLISHAMERICA, LLLP
www.publishamerica.com
Baltimore

Printed in the United States of America

CONTENTS

DEDICATION

This book was written for the individuals whom seem to be on the edge. To that person who feels like there is no hope, and about to give it all up. Understand how close you are to your healing, your greatest blessing, and your breakthrough.

Paul Harding High School basketball coach Al Gooden Sr. Thanks for caring for me and being patient enough to put up with me. I am very thankful to have had you as a coach; you were more like a father.

If you give up today, the same problem will be even more difficult tomorrow- DeVon D Cooper Sr.

INTRODUCTION

Let your story be told! Be the inspiration in someone's life. These are the goals of Jermaine Muff. A man who was once a boy determined to inspire through basketball, but was forced to make difficult adjustments. No excuses will be needed, Jermaine has been through the trial, and you can make it through what ever is standing in your way also. Keep your head up at all times.

HUMBLING SITUATIONS

What do you know about surprises?
Calm nights but harsh changes before sunrises
Darkness appear as you panic in fear
Loved ones gathered near, with tragedy tears

What do you know about facing your death?
Where the strong can't face their selves
Have you had the thoughts that life is pointless?
Unable to respond but hearing surrounding voices

Have you ever been there but feel physically separated
Fully clothed but feel spiritually naked
What do you know about being ashamed?
When it's you others feel is the shame

What you know about being the fool
A grown man i claim but can't tie my own shoes
What you know about having a stroke
Thinking with your life that's all she wrote
Being told to keep pushing but it's hard to find hope

Tell me what you live for
What do you know about how to endure?
Where do one find enough patience
What do you know about my humbling situations?

THE FINAL REBOUND

PRE-SEASON

Jermaine Muff was a young African-American boy trying to find himself, like any other young boy. He was born and raised in Fort Wayne, IN by his mother Janet Muff. Jermaine would watch days pass by while he played with his toys. Like most young boys, Jermaine didn't understand life at all, or why things had to be the way they were. Jermaine was close to his sisters, loved his family, and they all knew they needed a family bond to stay strong. They were in a very difficult situation as they watched their mother being incarcerated and endured nights of sleeping in cars. During an interview Jermaine stated Quote: (I remember going to school tired because of a lack of sleep, using motel restrooms to clean up before rushing off to school). Jermaine also surmised, that memories will keep him humble.

As a kid, Jermaine recognized the situation he and his family were dealing with, but he just didn't have a clue what to do about it.

Jermaine was a very comical young man. He was always finding reasons to laugh and crack jokes and was able to use school as a mental vacation. He needed this escapism to avoid the pains of the family demons of drug use, and the mysterious murder of his grandfather, whom he truly loved.

FIRST QUARTER

Jermaine's life would take a small turn in middle school, because something new was introduced to him. His classmates and teachers saw something in him that he couldn't see in himself. Jermaine was six feet, three inches tall in the sixth grade. They wanted the big man to play basketball for the school (Lake Side Middle), but he was not so interested. Finally Jermaine tried out for basketball and made the team because of his height and size. Sounds easy right? However, that was not the case, as Jermaine didn't have a bit of knowledge about basketball. Jermaine didn't know what a base line was to a chest pass. After a lot of help and hard work, he started to catch on to the game and even fell in love with the it.

While working on his new hobby and improving his basketball skills, he came across some significant mentors. The very first individual was his coach. Coach Causey seemed to care about Jermaine like a father would. He spent quality time encouraging the young boy and sharing his wisdom with Jemaine. Jermaine was humble, a good listener, and really wanted to learn. Coach Causey may not have realized the impact he had on Jermaine, but Jermaine truly appreciated coach Causey being strict on him. It made Jermaine work even harder knowing this coach truly believed in him.

A second individual was Mrs. Dorch, who taught Jermaine to stop making excuses. She wanted Jermaine to understand making people feel sorry for him wouldn't help him reach the goals he was striving for. Although he was the biggest student in the school, Jermaine was very playful and often in some type of trouble. As a result of that, Mrs. Dorch continued to work with him throughout his junior high school years.

Some people believe that it takes a village to raise a child. As Jermaine grew more mature as a young man, dealing with home issues, and continuing to grow in basketball, he was invited to some AAU basketball leagues. His very first team was in the SAC league called the Fort Wayne Fire. With this team, his confidence slowly increased. He had some good teammates and coaching, which helped him get better. Jermaine truly had a high level of respect for his coaching staff because of their loyalty. One coach helped take Jermaine's basketball game to the next level. He would pick him up for practice, movies, dinner, and spend quality time with him. This lead to Jermaine's boost of confidence and increased will to be better. Before Jermaine knew it, he was gaining some credibility and was offered a spot on the nationally known team called "Blessed In Jesus Name". This team was owned by well known sports agents Eugene Parker and Roosevelt Barnes.

On this nationally known team Jermaine would take his game to another level. He played against players like O.J. Mayo, Bill Walker, Kevin Love, Eric Gordon, Greg Oden, Mike Conely Jr. Daequan Cook, Glen (Big Baby) Davis, and many more including Jeffrey Jordan, the son of the great Michael Jordan.

SECOND QUARTER

Jermaine was now in the 8th grade and was a middle school star. He was getting a lot of hype and had high expectations going into high school. Although he was still dealing with family issues and a lot of stress, Jermaine tried his hardest to stay focused, and keep a good work ethic. The situation was a difficult one. Jermaine wound up living with the family of one of his basketball teammates. He was treated like he was really family and found a warm atmosphere and home. Although Jermaine was staying with this family and it was a good thing, he still worried about his family. At the time there was a lot going on in his life. Jermaine's grades were slipping, but by the time he was a sophomore in high school he was being recruited by the University of Illinois.

Many people would ask, what can be worse than people knowing your business and making jokes about it? What can be worse than sleeping in a car while being an up and coming basketball star? Jermaine got up for school one day and was ready for his basketball game; however, he felt dizzy and his eye sight was blurry. He went to the school nurse during school and she made him rest for about an hour. He felt better until game time, when he drank a Red Bull©. Jermaine was taken out of the game after he told his coach, Al Gooden, whom he had a lot of love for, that he wasn't feeling right.

After the game, the team showed Jermaine a lot of attention as he sat in the locker room zoned out. Jermaine Muff relayed, "I believe most people would have been fell out, but my will to fight whatever was happening to me kept me woke."

After moments passed by in the locker room, Jermaine couldn't fight any more. He collapsed from a stroke and all he could remember was the paramedics in the ambulance asking him his birth date and telling him to stay awake. Jermaine couldn't fight it any longer and thought it was time to die. Jermaine went into a semi coma for three days. He could feel pain and hear people talking, but he could not respond. Jermaine even heard people talking about him going into a nursing home if he lived.

Finally Jermaine woke up and all he could mumble was what happened to him and when would he be back on the basketball court. There were a lot of people around him, but no one could really understand what he was trying to say. People were crying and staring at him. He knew by the hesitation of the people that it was all over for him and the sport he loved. The doctor told everyone to clear the room and explained to Jermaine what happened and how he had experienced a serious brain stroke. Jermaine even heard a doctor requesting a nursing home, because he would never walk again. Now the doubt and internal questioning came into play. "If I live, where do I go from here? Do the people who say they love me truly mean it? If it's not basketball, what else can I be good at?"

As expected, it was a very long process of mental and physical recovery. Jermaine was released to go home and undergo therapy. The therapy really helped Jermaine rebuild faster than he expected. He was improving and starting to believe in himself again. Then, one night Jermaine was sitting in the house and began to feel a little weird, while talking on the phone. After hanging up the phone, he felt the same symptoms as when he had his previous stroke. He yelled out that he was having a stroke and his mom called the ambulance. The paramedics didn't believe he was having another one, so they gave him a few tests. A second stroke had come upon the seventeen year old, who now truly believed he wouldn't live to much longer.

When Jermaine was released from the hospital for the second time, he was in need of a lot of support and he got it. He had help from his uncle, Jerry Muff, and a guy by the name of Jim Winters, whom raised money for Jermaine. Jermaine never saw the money personally because of other family issues and hospital bills, but he truly appreciated Jim Winters.

Jermaine was confused and baffled as to why this happened to him. He went through therapy determined to get better, but after he saw how long it was taking, he was adamant on quitting. He was ready to give up and didn't care anymore if he lived or died.

THIRD QUARTER

While Jermaine was continuing to recover from the strokes, he started to spend a lot of time with some old school mates. He got his own apartment utilizing public housing assistance and let a couple of those friends move in. During this time he was introduced to a young lady named Jakaya Thomas through one of his friends. Originally, Jermaine wasn't into Jakaya at first, but eventually he started liking her and she became the mother of his daughter Kamiah Jordyn Muff, whom he loves more than anything or anyone besides God. A family was what Jermaine wanted, and they started to build together, as Jermaine was working on becoming a man.

As we all make mistakes, Jermaine made his own, trying to fit in and being perhaps too loyal to some people and things. Jermaine couldn't physically work, and he was not receiving any type of financial assistance. Although the baby was not born yet,

Jermaine needed to provide for his family and began selling drugs, and associating with gang members on a daily basis. The gang Jermaine was hanging out with had a reputation and a pretty big name in the city. After word got out that Jermaine was making a little money, someone robbed him. Guns were put to Jermaine's head and in his mouth. Jermaine was far from being fully recovered from the strokes and he could barely keep his own balance. That made it easy for the robbers to knock him down and stump him around the head and neck area. One guy even yelled out, let's put him in the bath tub and blow his brains out. One guy who seemed to be the leader, told the followers let's go, practically saving Jermaine's life.

The robbery scared Jermaine, but he felt he was a quitter if he stopped dealing drugs. He also felt he needed to be loyal to his friends. The tough part about peer pressure is being influenced by those who seem to be on top of the world. Jermaine was a weed smoker and a huge fan of the Scarface movie. He wanted to try cocaine and he did. He ended up doing cocaine for about a year. During that turbulent year in Jermaine's life, he ran the streets living a gangster's life. He mistreated the mother of his daughter and it took her threatening to leave him before reality hit him. He was embarrassed by the fact that he was getting high off coke and people were starting to find out about it. Things were starting to get hot for the former basketball player and his friends, as Jermaine's apartment got raided by the law, he went to jail, and served time on house arrest.

Jermaine started to realize that his life was controlling him rather than him controlling his own life. He wanted to see change in his life for himself and the people who loved him. He lost friends because he didn't want to be in the company of people who wanted to sit around getting high.

After friends became victims of several homicides, Jermaine realized he had been trying to substitute something for basketball and he had no hope, because basketball was no more.

FOURTH QUARTER

Now that Jermaine's eyes were opened, he wanted something good, but he just didn't know what it was going to be. He was humbled after all that had happened so quick in his young life. He went to drug abuse counseling and started to visit churches, trying to find himself.

Trusting that God would give him the direction he needed, Jermaine finally got his prayer answered. He ran into an old classmate several times who was the brother of one of the biggest drug dealers in his past crew. They were happy to see each other every time, but it was all happy with hugs and see you later. This guy was different from his brother in so many ways, as he was the type to build businesses and was happily married with children. Jermaine called him one day asking about how he could get his business started. The conversation was far different than what Jermaine expected, as DeVon D. Cooper

Sr. also known as Duke, set a meeting with Jermaine.

In the Starbucks© meeting, Jermaine was informed that business was not a hustle. He was told that business was a brand built by a team or individual with a divine purpose to help others and make money. Cooper had Jermaine's undivided attention as he kept talking about having a vision. He said, "Vision was the plan and process to accomplish the purpose." Before the meeting ended, Cooper told Jermaine to stay in touch and to work on taking his drive to a level he had never experienced. During this time, Jermaine was staying with his uncle Jerry in a six figure home. He started to spend a lot of time with DeVon Cooper and grew increasingly more focused on building his business and caring for his daughter.

From then on, Jermaine continued to grow wiser as a man, separating himself from those who couldn't and/or wouldn't help him. Jermaine saw the faith DeVon Cooper had in God and the blessings he was receiving and that helped increase Jermaine's faith astronomically. DeVon Cooper got Jermaine to really acknowledge what God had done in his life to help him become a stronger and wiser individual. According to Jermaine, "DeVon Cooper has helped me with my speech and professionalism, how to deal with family issues, and even got him to remove a dollar sign tattoo from under his eye." Jermaine went on building a solid foundation with and for his daughter and started a vending machine company. He also started other companies and began to travel around the nation to experience bigger things.

Words of Jermaine Muff:

I am so blessed to be living and I realize, I am living to be a blessing for others. I am not only focused on bettering myself and my family, but also contributing to improving millions of lives worldwide. I want to take the passion I had in basketball and use it for changing lives. I may not ever jump or run on a basketball court again, but I have rebounded in life. I have met some wonderful people and I appreciate the good that has been a part of my breathing days. I've been hurt, but I'm healed. I've been talked about, but I can talk again. I've been betrayed, but I'm loyal. I was supposed to be in a group home, but I have my own business. I was supposed to be dead, but I live and Christ lives in me. I am filled with love, and no strife or bitterness will conquer my heart. I am a father, a friend, a business man, God's witness, and I'm somebody. This is my final rebound, what's yours? You have not lived life until you have appreciated it.